Tales of a SIXTH-GRADE MUPPET

Story and Art by
KIRK SCROGGS

Bath • New York • Singapore • Hong Kong • Cologne • Delhi
Melbourne • Amsterdam • Johannesburg • Auckland • Shenzhen

First edition published by Parragon in 2012
Parragon
Queen Street House
4 Queen Street
Bath BA1 1HE, UK
www.parragon.com

Designed by: Jim Willmott
Edited by: Katrina Hanford
Production by: Jack Aylward

ISBN 978-1-4454-5824-3

Printed in China

CHAPTER

1

The Great Gonzo:
My Hero, Everybody's Hero
by Danvers Blickensderfer

Chandle light fixture ← blankie ← blast off!

Ever since the time I broke out of my crib using a baby bottle and my blue blankie, I have dreamed of being a world-famous escape artist. So, naturally, when Mr. Piffle asked us to write about our heroes, many of my ~~colleag~~ ~~colleegs~~ friends said "you should pick ~~Harry~~ Houdini! With his daring escapes and manly loincloths, he's the greatest escape artist ever!" Right?
Oh contraire!

SHACKLES
Tank of water

I say Harry Houdini isn't fit to share the same strait-jacket with The Great Gonzo, my alltime idol and hero.
What makes Gonzo so danged special? Well, for starters, he has "Great" in his name. Have you ever heard of "Houdini the great" or "Ryan Seacrust the great"? I didn't think so.

Viva el Flaco!

Gonzo's famed flaming Tambourine Chicken jump, Buenos Aires, 1993.

Gonzo is a world re-nouned daredevil, stuntman, singer, actor, super model, and all around ringmaster of the wack-a-doodle. His charity work on the

© Danvers Blickensderfer

"Feed the Chickens" concert since 2008 has once won him accolades all over the world.

I've seen every movie Gonzo has ever made five hundred times including Muppet Treasure Island, Muppets from Space, and the little known cult classic Gonzo vs. Arachnoturkey.

I even dress up as Gonzo for Halloween each year, as well as other special occasions.

Here's me at last year's Halloween ball

Here I am at Aunt Patty's wedding.

And at my great uncle Barny's funeral.

In concusion, it is abundantly clear that Gonzo is truly the greatest entertainer to ever live and, therefore, my hero. He should be your hero, too.

Please discuss amongst yourselves.

This groundbreaking Gonzo report took me three days and two ballpoint pens to write. And, just so you know, I do all my own artwork, so it's copyrighted to me, Danvers Blickensderfer. Don't get any ideas about photocopying it and turning it in as your own.

After I finished reading my report to the class, I could tell by the stunned silence that they loved it.

"Uh... thank you, Danvers," said Mr Piffle slowly. "I'll add this to the binder with your previous reports, 'Gonzo: An American Icon', 'Gonzo: Defender of Freedom' and, of course, your series of tempera paintings, *Gonzo: Still Life in Motion*." (You maybe have noticed that I'm a bit of a Gonzo fanatic. I meant everything I said in that report and then some. I even have a Gonzo T-shirt for every day of the week... except for Sundays. That's my disco pirate day.)

Before Mr Piffle could call on another student, I announced, "At this time, I would like to perform my grand finale!"

Mr Piffle frowned. "Uh, oral reports don't generally have grand finales."

But it was too late – the wheels of fate were in motion.

"And now, in tribute to The Great Gonzo, I shall balance a basket of free-range emu eggs on my chin, using this yardstick, to the tune of 'Bingo Was His Name-O!'"

The stunt was going beautifully. The class was cheering and shrieking with excitement... or fear (I couldn't be sure which one because I was kinda busy balancing the eggs), until...

...something went wrong. I must have misjudged the yardstick-to-chin lateral shiftitude, because the next thing I knew, I had an emu-egg scramble on my noggin.

Mr Piffle wasn't pleased. "I hope you're happy, Mr Blickensderfer. For your punishment, I want you to sit down and listen to your classmates' reports with egg on your face."

There was no getting around it: This embarrassing

incident was going to make my life at school miserable. (Not that it was going gangbusters before this.) It was bad enough having a name like Danvers. I mean, really, who names their kid Danvers?

My parents swear they got it from one of their favourite books.

After the bell rang, I met up in the hall with my best friend, Pasquale. I asked him if word of my humiliation had already gotten around.

"'Fraid so," said Pasquale. "I already read about it on the bathroom wall."

Pasquale wouldn't lie. He has been a faithful assistant and the official safety officer for all of my front-yard stunt shows since the second grade... not to mention a thorough reader of bathroom-wall news items.

He's a lot smarter than me – we're talking straight B's here – but he sure has a limited vocabulary. All he ever says is "This seems unsafe, this seems unsafe," over and over, like a broken record. Occasionally he'll mix it up and say something like "Could you call 911?" or "Is it normal for my ankle to be purple?"

Last month, his folks made me sign a waiver before they'd let him help me with any more stunts. It probably had something to do with him coming home one night soaked in tapioca pudding and missing a tooth....

I guess there *is* a certain level of risk associated with my stunts.

Like a lot of folks, his mum and dad just don't get it – true art involves sacrifice! Vincent van Gogh gave up his ear, the Sphinx in Egypt is missing her nose and I once lost my lunch after eating a whole pint of creamed spinach in time with "Yankee Doodle Dandy."

In the words of Gonzo: If it doesn't leave a mess, it isn't art.

CHAPTER 2

The 207th annual
BLOCK CITY

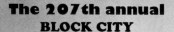

FALL ON ICE FESTIVAL

WITH WORLD CHAMPION
SKATER TURK GIBLETT

FEATURING

BLOCK CITY MAYOR
MARGE MERGER

SUAVE
WEATHERMAN
AUSTIN SHOWERS

CRAZY MO
FROM CRAZY MO'S
BEARD TRIMMER
EMPORIUM

WITH

THE FLUFFLEBERRIES

AND TIME PERMITTING,
ACTRESS MERYL SKREEP

TRYOUTS TODAY!

Unfazed by my report-related,

egg-smeared, bathroom-wall–reported debacle at school, I convinced Pasquale to head over to the school auditorium so I could audition for the Block City Fall on Ice Festival. Each school in the area was getting five minutes in the show to present their best and brightest talents – who would then perform on the ice.

"We've got this in the bag," I told Pasquale as we unpacked our vintage boom box and a huge whiteboard. "These other kids are so plain vanilla. Our act will set this place on fire!"

"Students!" said Mrs Grumbles, the drama teacher. "Before we begin the auditions, I have an exciting surprise for you. I present to you our special guest judge, taxied in just for the Fall on Ice tryouts. Without further ado, I give you... Miss Piggy!"

I couldn't believe my eyes. The one and only Miss Piggy was going to hear my pitch and judge me – as she had judged so many in the past.

"All right, cut the chatter!" called Piggy. "Let's get this party started! I've gotta shoot a Celebrity Eyebrow Threading advert at two thirty!"

Miss Piggy was honest, forthright and direct with contestants. In other words: She was brutal.

The time had come – it was finally my turn. "Ladies and gentlemen," I began. "I'd like to present my ultimate stunt: *En Hommage à Gran Gonzo*! Hit the music, Pasquale!"

Pasquale blasted some dramatic classical music from the stereo and I laid out my proposal, step-by-step.

"Picture, if you will, in the middle of the ice rink, a bouncy castle filled with ninjas. Ninjas that are gyrating with razor-laced hula hoops! It's a vision of horror!

"Then I, the Daring Danvers, leap into the fray on my pogo stick, dodging the shimmying shinobis while tooting the 'Hymn of the Royal Canadian Mounties' on my French horn with just one hand!

"All the while, my esteemed assistant, Pasquale, will slowly overinflate the bouncy castle until…"

Pasquale switched off the classical music, swapped out the CD, and pressed play again so that the sound of a huge explosion filled the auditorium —

"…we reach our dramatic conclusion. Thank you, Pasquale."

"*Moi* can appreciate your artistic reach, but that

sounds just plain crazy, kid," said Miss Piggy.

My dreams were crushed. Even Miss Piggy had rejected me. It was almost too much to bear.

But then, something happened. As Pasquale and I collected our presentation materials and walked off the stage, all the girls in the room shrieked with glee and barrelled up the aisle towards Pasquale and me.

But the screeching horde of girls ran right over our scrawny hides on their way to the stage. I looked back to see my worst nightmare: Coldrain Middle School's most popular boy band, Emo Shun, was ready to perform. The band members were fellow sixth graders: the three-foot-tall Cody Carter, the French-speaking Danny Enfant and the lead singer Kip Strummer. They even had their own sappy, schmaltzy music video online for their new single, "Hey Girl."

Kip strummed his guitar and said, "Yo, this first song goes out to you, girl."

"*Moi?*" asked Miss Piggy.

Danny Enfant repeated everything Kip said in French to Miss Piggy.

When their song was over, Miss Piggy didn't even bat an eyelash before she announced, "Auditions are over! Emo Shun will be representing Coldrain Middle School at the Fall on Ice spectacular! *Moi* has spoken."

Dinner that night was miserable and I'm not just talking about the slimy meat loaf Mum was serving. Not only were my parents totally not on my side, but my little sister, Chloe, was rubbing it in as usual.

"Don't worry, bwudda," she said, grinning. "Now you'll have pwenty of fwee time to pwactise being a loser. Heyooo!"

Don't be fooled by Chloe's sweet, adorable voice and cuddly looks. She is evil.

With Chloe's cackling taunts still ringing in my ears, I tromped upstairs. What I needed was a good, healthy sulk in my bedroom with the one friend who would stand by me, no matter what: my pet rat, Curtis.

Yes, sir, if it wasn't for Curtis I don't know what I'd do at times like th—

"Is this annoying you, big bwudda? huh? is it? is it? huh?"

Okay. So, that annoying sound was coming from my little sister. And yes, you have just discovered my greatest humiliation of all: I share bunk beds with Chloe. Can you imagine if this ever got out to the other kids at school? Well, you don't have to imagine, because Chloe already blabbed about it on the bus.

Oh, well. At least I got the top bunk.

As I looked up at the Gonzo and Muppet posters that covered my ceiling, I felt my self-pity well up.

"Oh, Gonzo. Will I ever be as talented and fearless as you?" I asked.

I set my alarm, tucked Curtis in, rolled over and closed my eyes. "I wish I were like you, Gonzo," I whispered.

ZZZZZ...

I was awakened by a bright green flash – like the kind you get when a glow stick explodes (don't ask how I know that) – and a zappy buzzing sound.

Glancing around the room, I thought everything seemed to be normal. It was still dark. I looked over at my alarm clock to see what time it was.

"Twelve twenty-two," I mumbled, half-asleep. "I can

still get back to that dream I was having."

And what an awesome dream it was.

I was running towards a tall, round building that looked like Gonzo's head! The members of Emo Shun were chasing me, their awful "Hey Girl" song echoing throughout the land.

The ground was soft and green, like felt. A huge hill rose up in front of me and rolled under me like a swell in the ocean. As I crossed Gonzo's nose, I saw a door. Kermit the Frog was the doorman and he was ushering me in.

Then I woke up again. My alarm was blaring and sunlight was pouring into the room, brighter than usual.

The clock said 7:02 am. I could hear Chloe snoring like an old man with asthma underneath me. That's my sister – just adorable.

Curtis gave a little squeaky yawn and stretch and opened his beady eyes. He blinked at me suddenly and his eyes nearly bugged out of his skull. You would have thought he was looking at a zombie pirate with worms pouring out of its ears. Curtis squeaked and jumped into an empty Cheezy-Qs bag that I had left on my bed.

"What's your problem?" I asked, reaching for the trembling bag.

i wobbled over to the bathroom and reached up to grab the knob. my hands were having the darnedest time turning it.

curtis was still looking at me like I was a stranger.

i finally got the door open and walked over to the mirror above the sink, only to discover...

Staring back at me was... well, it was me, but... I was really brightly coloured. My nose was like a red squishy ball. My hair was more blonde than usual, like canary feathers. I had a huge mouth and my eyes were really big and bugged out. The super-skinny arms poking out of my sleeves reminded me of someone... but who? That's when I noticed the Kermit design on my Muppet shower curtain.

"Holy Toledo! I'm... I'm a Muppet!" I screamed.

There was only one thing to do...

My little sis sat up like a bear cub rudely awakened from hibernation. She rubbed her eyes sleepily.

She dropped her hands and stared at me.

"Stay back! Stay back!" she shouted. "I'll use my craft scissors on you!"

"It's me, Chloe! Your brother!"

Knock! Knock! Knock!

We froze when we heard Mum's voice on the other side of the door.

is everything okay in there?
i heard horrendous screams and threats of bodily harm involving craft scissors.

"It's okay, Mum," I yelled through the door. "We were just re-enacting Chloe's favourite scene from *Cinderella*!"

I grabbed Chloe by the shoulders. "You can't tell Mum and Dad about this! Promise me!"

"Why not?" Chloe cried.

"Because, knowing Mum, she'll take me to some quack doctor!"

"What's in it for me, Megamouth?" Chloe snarked. I looked around the room and sighed. "Okay. Help me keep this a secret until it wears off and I'll let you hang two Fluffleberries posters in place of two of my Gonzos."

"Deal!" she said. "The first thing you'll need is a disguise if you wanna make it through breakfast."

CHAPTER

"**Why do you have a towel wrapped** around your head?" Mum asked as I sat eating breakfast in my brilliant disguise. "And are you wearing my silk bathrobe?"

"I'm giving my pores a deep steam cleanse," I said. "Sometimes you just gotta treat yourself."

"Well, treat yourself to some soggy cereal," Mum said, slapping a bowl of Dreeri-Os onto the table and giving me a weird glance. "Your mouth looks bigger."

I ignored the comment and shovelled cereal into my new giant flip-top mouth.

"Mum," I said, "I think I'm destined to stay home today. I'm not feelin' it."

She frowned and said, "Then you're also destined to visit Doctor Coughka."

"But Mum!"

"Nope." She shook her head. "It's either school or thermometers and needles! Now go get ready."

Upstairs, I was a nervous wreck.

"What am I gonna do?" I cried. "I can't go to school looking like a mummy from the bed and bath barn!"

"Settle down, bobblehead!" Chloe said. "I got another idea. But it's gonna cost you four more gonzo posters."

So I headed to the bus stop with Chloe, in an even more ingenious disguise – my old astronaut costume from our school play, *Alien Infestation: The Musical*.

My wobbly space suit certainly turned heads. While we waited at the corner bus stop, something weird happened. Two old men pulled up in a convertible and started making fun of me. For no reason!

I recognized the sound of the merciless insults.

"That's Statler and Waldorf!" I said. "They always

torture poor Fozzie Bear on *The Muppet Show*. But why are they bothering me?"

"I don't know, but I like them," said Chloe.

"Hey!" Statler yelled. "Buzz Lightyear called. He wants his outfit back! Ha ha ha!"

"And one more thing..." added Waldorf. "When you get to Saturn... be sure to give us a ring! Ha ha ha!"

Then, as quickly as they'd appeared, they sped off, laughing.

Everyone at school – teachers and students alike – was pretty shocked to see me roaming the school halls dressed as an astronaut. Pasquale was the only one who didn't bat an eye. I guess once you've witnessed your best friend juggling holiday hams dressed as Gonzo in a glow-in-the-dark tutu for Groundhog Day 2008, nothing surprises you.

Mr Piffle tried to force me to take my outfit off, but I wouldn't budge.

Mr Mallard, our school counsellor, tried a different method to get me to take it off.

An unexpected bonus was that the suit was good protection from Greevus Snipply, the walking germ incubator.

It was going to take a lot more than pleading

teachers to get me to take that space suit off. Namely, a large, hurtling projectile.

You see, P.E. with Coach Kraft was my next class, and the two of us didn't exactly get along. Through the years, he'd been responsible for some of my most painful school memories.

Coach Kraft tried to tell me that I was legally obliged to change into my gym clothes before playing dodgeball. I told him that I was just exercising my Thirtieth Amendment right to dress as a heroic astronaut anytime I chose.

Luckily, Coach thought an amendment is something you do to a pair of pants that don't fit, so he let me play dodgeball in my costume. Let me tell you, it was quite a workout! My scrawny new Muppet body was having a hard time carrying around that heavy suit, but I was playing pretty well. Better than ever, actually.

Then I heard some voices calling from the sidelines.

It was Statler and Waldorf again, sitting in the bleachers this time. They were starting to get on my nerves.

"Go pick on someone your own age!" I yelled.

"We would, but it's not polite to make fun of the dead! Ha ha!"

Thanks to those old curmudgeons, I let my guard down and got pegged. The blow knocked my helmet off and I landed flat on my back.

Everyone gathered around what looked like my headless body.

"Coach, you told me to put a little attitude in my throw," said Kip.

"Yeah, but I didn't mean for you to knock his head off!" explained the coach.

"Wait a minute!" said Kip. "He's moving!"

"Just nerves," said Coach Kraft. "A chicken with no head can still run around for up to thirty seconds. I've seen it happen."

"I'm gonna be sick," moaned Pasquale.

This was it. It was time to come out of my shell and reveal the new me. The students in my P.E. class went nuts, screaming and shrieking. Coach Kraft clutched his chest like he was having the big one.

"Who are you, dude?" asked Kip. "Where's Danvers?"

"It's me. I'm Danvers."

"Don't be ridiculous!" yelled Coach. "Danvers doesn't have a squishy red nose and a crazy yellow mop top!"

"I promise it's me," I said. "When I woke up this morning, I just wasn't myself. Pasquale, you know it's me, right?"

Even Pasquale was sceptical.

I breathed a sigh of relief. Everyone was happy that my head was still attached. Kip and Pasquale helped me up and out of my astronaut suit.

"You should have just told me," said Pasquale.

"I know, but how do you tell people you went through a Muppetmorphosis?" I asked.

"I'm not people. I'm your best friend," he said.

"You're right." I nodded. "That's what Gonzo would have done. He embraces his weirdness and so should I!"

CHAPTER 5

i can't believe you didn't tell us.
we would have rushed you to the doctor first thing.
what is this slop?

"**I**t's my fault," Mum said at dinner, sniffling over another horrific meat loaf. "I never should have exposed you to years of craft projects. All that felt and sewing."

"Don't be ridiculous," said Dad. "It was my fault. I let him watch too much Muppets. He shoulda been watching football and senseless violence."

"May I be excused?" I said. They were really bumming me out.

I tried to relax in my room, but fabric-nibbling Curtis was becoming a little too fond of my new look.

I looked up at my ceiling full of Fluffleberries posters... uh, wait... and one Gonzo poster.

"Gonzo, what should I do? You have so much experience dealing with being unique, one of a kind, a...whatever. Please help me. Send me a sign."

Suddenly, I heard a faint, muffled voice. It was coming from the closet!

"Gonzo? Is that you?" I asked. "Are you trying to

speak to me?"

I climbed down off the bunk bed, darted across the room and flung open the closet door to hear my sister on the phone.

"That's right. He transformed last night. If we make the deal, I want sixty per cent and foreign distribution rights."

"I can't believe it!" I yelled. "My own sister plans to sell my story!"

"Look, you're one of a kind, big brother. We gotta capitalize on that before someone else does. I just got off the phone with Harry Beardstein and he said he would green-light a deal in a heartbeat."

"Green light!" I shouted. "A green light! That's it!"

It was all coming back to me now: what happened the night of my transformation. My brain was racing. I had to discover the source of that green flash. Only then would I unravel the mystery of my Muppetmorphosis!

The next morning, Mum took me to see a bunch of doctors. Unfortunately, not one of them could explain how my transformation could have occurred.

At lunchtime, Mum swung by the drive-thru at the Bulgy Burger for some grub. On our way out of the lot, I saw something fantastic.

There before us stood the answer to my prayers: Veterinarian's Hospital. If Dr Bob couldn't help us, no one could. It took some doing to get Mum to let me go in, but she finally caved.

After a short wait in the lobby, I was called in by a groovy hippie nurse – it was Janice from The Electric Mayhem Band!

The nurse took me down a long hall filled with patients.

"I'm, like, Nurse Janice, man," she said. Sitting on a bench in the hall was my worst nightmare – Statler and Waldorf, dressed in hospital gowns. I just couldn't get away from those guys.

"Ignore those old dudes. They're just trying to freak you out," said Nurse Janice, taking me into a freezing-cold room. "If you could, like, strip down to your underwear, that would be cool."

"How's it goin', kid?" came a voice from behind me. It was Dr Bob. Nurse Piggy was close behind. The doctor shut the door and pulled out a clipboard.

"Aren't you really Rowlf the Dog?" I asked.

"Nope. Dr Bob's the name. Keeping folks in stitches is my game."

"Dr Bob," said Janice, "this is far out. Like, this kid says that he went to bed a sixth-grade boy and woke up a sixth-grade Muppet!"

"Hmmm. I woke up a Muppet this morning, too!"

"Really?" I asked. "What happened?"

"He wouldn't get out of bed!"

"Ha ha ha!" The nurses laughed.

I shook my head. "I'm serious. Ever since I changed, I swear I've been seeing stuff that should only exist on TV."

"Like what, pray tell?" said Dr Bob.

"Like this place. Your name is really Rowlf, and you play a doctor on TV. And those two old guys out in the hall that keep pestering me. And then there's you, Miss Piggy," I continued. "You're a famous actress. Why are you working at Veterinarian's Hospital?"

"Even the most famous actresses must research their upcoming roles," said Piggy.

"I guess you could say her career has gone to the dogs!" joked Dr Bob.

When the examination (and the onslaught of jokes) was finally over, Dr Bob asked me to get dressed. Then he sat me and my mum down for a serious discussion.

"If you really want to reverse this Muppetmorphosis, I say look up scientific genius and bane of lab assistants Dr Bunsen Honeydew. He may not be able to help, but it will certainly advance the plot."

Of course! The famous Dr Bunsen Honeydew of the world-renowned Muppet Labs! He might have the answers I was seeking. I was going to have to find this scientific pioneer. And I was going to need some help to do it.

CHAPTER 6

After we got home I ran over to Pasquale's house and banged on his bedroom window. After a few seconds the window opened.

"What are you doing here?" moaned Pasquale, who was wrapped in a blanket and looked like a hundred-year-old peasant woman with a shawl. "Aren't you supposed to be at school?"

"I was gonna ask you the same question, my friend," I said.

"I called in sick," he said with a sniffle. "My glands are discombobulated."

Pasquale calls in sick about once a week. I'm not sure if even half the ailments he comes down with actually exist, but they usually involve the word "discombobulated."

I invited myself in and crawled through his window. "Get dressed, *kemo sabe*. I'm a man on a mission, and you are now, officially, the Watson to my Sherlock, the Wendy to my Peter Pan, the twice-baked potato to my—"

"You need to use my computer, don't you?" Pasquale sighed.

"Yep!" I said, jumping on his laptop. "It'll just take a second."

"What are you looking for?" asked Pasquale.

"Not a what, but a who," I said. "Dr Bunsen Honeydew, world-famous scientist from Muppet Labs, associate of The Great Gonzo and winner of the 2002 Cowbell Peace Prize in Science for his 'Isn't Science Nifty?' theorem.

"Now, watch as I go into the Internet and retrieve all data on this elusive charac—"

"Here, let me do it," said Pasquale, grabbing the keyboard. "You're just punching random keys until I do it for you anyway."

Pasquale quickly found a webpage chock-full of info.

"There he is!" I cried, pointing at the screen. "Wow, it says here that Dr Bunsen Honeydew is teaching science for a limited time as a special guest at the Eagle Talon Academy of Fine Arts.... It's a school for 'budding youngsters driven by the urge to perform.' That's me! Come on," I said. "If we hop on our bikes now, we can get there before class lets out!"

To get into the Eagle Talon Academy, we had to first meet with Sam the Eagle, the principal of the joint. Sam was serious about everything and very, very patriotic. Pasquale and I had agreed that we would pretend to be prospective foreign-exchange students.

"My friend Herbert here is from Bangladesh," I said. "My name's Chauncey and I sailed all the way from, uh...Idaho."

"Ah, Idaho – a charming locale. One of my top fifty favourite states in the United States of America. Ahem!" Sam coughed. "Now, let's get down to brass tacks. Eagle Talon Academy is a school with integrity, a school with proper values, a school with principles."

"Don't all schools have principals?" I interrupted him.

Sam gave me a serious stare that made me pretty sure he hadn't laughed since 1974. "Was that a joke of some sort, young man? Because if it was, I must warn you, we will not accept tomfoolery at Eagle Talon."

Ever since my Muppetmorphosis, I had started to make lots of puns and witty comebacks, even in the most uncomfortable situations. I couldn't help it.

Pasquale convinced Sam the Eagle not to throw us out. "He didn't mean any offense, Mr The Eagle. I think it was just a simple misunderstanding."

"As I was saying," continued Sam, "I started this academy to give America's youth a proper education in the fine arts so they can go on to a distinguished career at the Muppet Theatre."

Our tour began with a stop by the lockers, where a group of students was hanging out.

"Children, these are two prospective students. Please extend a warm Eagle Talon salutation to them," said Sam.

Suddenly, an eerie, gibberish-sounding song echoed through the hall: *"Yørn desh børn, der ritt gitt der gue..."*

"This place makes our school look downright normal," whispered Pasquale.

"Why is Swedish Chef working here?" I asked.

"Oh, he replaced our old lunch lady when she went missing," said a pink girl frog who had walked up to us, along with a tall girl wearing a long ponytail. "My name's Ingy and this is Minette."

"Say, you ladies wouldn't know where to find the science lab, would you?" I asked.

"Oh, you're looking for Dr Honeydew?" said Ingy. "Sure. Straight down the hall, just past the vending machine. Oh, and one little word of advice: Don't agree to help him with any experiments, no matter how politely he asks. Bye!"

As we approached Dr Honeydew's

As we approached Dr Honeydew's laboratory door, I whispered to Pasquale, "Isn't it weird? Everything's all mixed up. I'm a Muppet, Statler and Waldorf are stalking me, Dr Bob runs a real hospital and now the Swedish Chef and Dr Honeydew are here at a private school run by Sam the Eagle – it's nuts!"

We knocked and then opened Dr Honeydew's door.

Inside, the place was filled with glass test tubes, which were bubbling over with toxic fluids. In the middle of the room, a bald man wearing glasses and a lab coat was performing an experiment on his tall, bulging-eyed, flaming-haired assistant.

oh, greetings, children! Beaker and I were just exploring a safer, science-friendly method of popping corn.

meep!

"Dr Honeydew, is that you?" I asked, dodging the popcorn shrapnel that was shooting all over the place.

"Yes, my dear friends," said the doctor as he blasted his partner with a fire extinguisher. "Come in, come in. This is my lab assistant, Beaker. Say hello, Beaker."

"Meep!" meeped Beaker, smoke drifting out of his ears. He looked kinda like a breadstick with ping-pong-ball eyes and a bright orange mop top.

"Um, Dr Honeydew," I said, "don't you have a lab at the Muppet Theatre? Why are you at this school?"

"Mee moo moo," cried Beaker as he turned away.

"That is a sensitive subject," said Honeydew, patting Beaker on the back. "This is a temporary location. We had a minor mishap at our lab involving four gallons of explosive liquids, an angry rhinoceros beetle and Beaker's nose."

I quickly filled him in on my predicament. When I mentioned the part about seeing a green flash in the middle of the night, his eyes lit up – well, if he had eyes they would have lit up.

"What time on Wednesday did you say you witnessed the flash of green?" he asked.

"At twelve twenty-two AM. Why?"

Dr Honeydew pulled out a huge leather-bound book and said, "If my suspicion is correct... Yes, look here! This is a logbook of every experiment that we have conducted. Beaker was taking detailed notes that evening. If you look closely, at twelve twenty-two am he wrote 'MEEP!' "

"What were you guys working on so late at night?" I asked.

"If memory serves, we were test-firing the new extremely high-powered laser that I designed to cure dry, sun-damaged hair. I call it the Scalp Hair Analyzer and Moisturizing Plutonium Ultrasonic Zapatron, or SHAMPUZ for short.

"At twelve twenty-two am I was testing the device on Beaker here, when it exploded, sending a stray energy beam straight through the ceiling and into the night sky. Such are the vagaries of science. Guess what colour that energy beam was?"

"Chartreuse?" guessed Pasquale.

"It was bright green!" said Honeydew.

I was super-excited. "Just like the flash I saw before I transformed!" I said. "Do you suppose that stray laser could have struck me in my bed and caused the Muppetmorphosis?"

"Well, ever since I saw Miss Piggy play a little orphan girl on Broadway, I've learned that anything is possible, no matter how unbelievable or frightening."

"Is there any way you could reverse the effects?" I asked.

"I tell you what," Honeydew replied. "Beaker and I will rebuild that damaged laser and retest it to see if it caused your condition. In fact, we won't rest until we have that dangerous contraption up and running once more. Isn't that right, Beaker?"

We said our farewells to the good doctor and the not-feeling-so-good Beaker.

We made a dash down the hall to the exit, hoping not to run into Sam the Eagle again on our way out.

That's when I caught a glimpse of something out of the corner of my eye. Something life-altering.

Hanging on a big bulletin board with a bunch of ads was the greatest flyer I've ever seen.

Hey, kids!
Announcing the first annual
MUPPET
AFTER-SCHOOL INTERNSHIP
Learn these valuable life skills with the pros:

COMEDY!

BEING A TEAM PLAYER

Inner peace through meditation

CONSTRUCTIVE CRITICISM

Just send in a two-page essay about your favorite Muppet!
Deadline: October 2nd

"Pasquale, I could turn in that essay I wrote about Gonzo!" I shouted, exploding with excitement. "Imagine – I could work for the one and only Kermit the Frog. Or maybe, just maybe, I could fetch bandages for The Great Gonzo! This is it, Pasquale! My big chance! My dream! I'm gonna get that internship and nothing is going to stop me!"

"Dude," said Pasquale, pointing at the bottom of the poster. "The deadline was two days ago."

I was devastated. I felt like I was on a rocket to happiness that just got hit by anti-aircraft fire.

CHAPTER

8

blech!

At dinner I was too bummed
out to even complain about my mum's meat loaf. I put a forkful in my mouth and chewed.

Mum tried to comfort me. "I'm sure you'll get another chance to work with the Muppets."

Dad held up an envelope and said, "The Muppets? They sent Danvers a letter."

I jumped across the table to snatch the letter from Dad and read it aloud.

Dear Danvers,

We are pleased to inform you that your entry in the Muppet Essay Contest was a winner. Yaaaay! We would like to offer you an internship position! Please report to the Muppet Theatre tomorrow after school.

Amphibiously yours,
Kermit the Frog

P.S. That little sister of yours deserves a big hug!

"I didn't even submit an essay. This is crazy!" I looked at my sister. "What did you do?"

"Have you been up to something, Chloe?" asked Mum.

My parents took a look at her essay and within three seconds, Mum was crying. "Oh, Danvers, just look at what Chloe did for you. It's so precious."

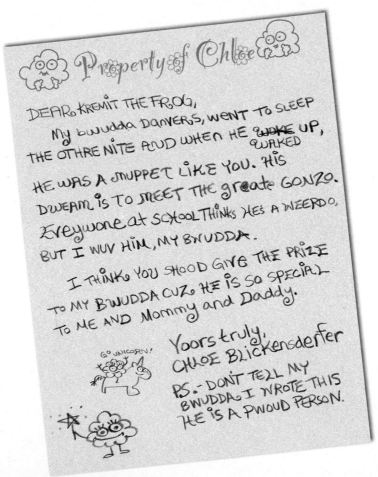

Property of Chloe

DEAR KREMIT THE FROG,

My bwudda DANVERS, WENT TO SLEEP THE OTHRE NITE AND WHEN HE ~~WOKE~~ UP, ~~QWAKED~~

HE WAS A MUPPET LIKE YOU. HIS DWEAM IS TO MEET THE greate GONZO. Eveywone at scXool THInKs HES A WEERDO, BUT I WUV HIM, MY BWUDDA.

I THINK YOU SHOOD GIVE THE PRIZE TO MY BWUDDA CUZ HE IS SO SPECIAL TO ME AND Mommy and Daddy.

GO UNICORN!

Yoors truly,
CHLOE BLICKENSderfer

P.S. - DON'T TELL MY BWUDDA I WROTE THIS HE IS A PWOUD PERSON.

I was stunned and amazed.

She had to be up to no good.

That night I decided to do something crazy. I thanked my sister. It hurt, let me tell you, but I did it.

The next day at school, I told Pasquale the good news. He had a hard time believing Chloe had done something nice for me, too, even if it did involve a healthy profit.

"You realize this is the same Chloe who posted a video of you in your Spider-Man undies, singing 'Skip to My Lou'?" he asked.

But I didn't care what her motives were – I was going to be an intern at the Muppet Theatre!

Despite my good mood, the day seemed to drag on forever. The hour hand on that darned clock seemed like it was covered in tar. I just counted the seconds until...

CHAPTER

Well, that's my ride," I said, **staring** at the magic mystery bus waiting in front of the school.

"Welcome aboard the crazy train," said the driver. "I'm Dr Teeth, your captain of the cosmos, your misconducting conductor, your act of nature with the toothy nomenclature. Over there is Zoot on the sax, there's Floyd on the bass, in the back that's Animal on drums and I believe you've met Janice on the ax."

I sat down next to a kid pig who looked very familiar. It was a student from the Eagle Talon Academy.

"Hey, Hockney! So you must be the other winner of the essay contest," I said.

"Yes," he answered. "I'm not used to sharing the spotlight. Driver, please step on it!"

Suddenly, Animal started chanting something behind us.

POTHOLE! POTHOLE! POTHOLE!

I leaned forwards and asked Dr Teeth, "What's he going on about?"

"Dead Man's Pothole is up ahead," said Dr Teeth, tightening his seat belt. "It's Animal's favourite. Here we go, everybody!" Dr Teeth put the pedal to the metal and drove the bus over the biggest pothole this side of the Grand Canyon.

The bus hit the hole so hard, everybody launched into the air. I almost hit the roof. It was like riding a rickety old roller coaster, except cheaper and less safe!

Dr Teeth stopped the bus, turned to us and said, "Is everybody okay?"

"Yes," Hockney whined as I helped him back into his seat. "Thank you for asking."

Then Dr Teeth shifted his gear stick and shouted, "All right! Let's do it in reverse!!!"

When we arrived at the theatre, Kermit ushered us into the backstage area. The joint was hopping with all sorts of crazy acts – juggling chickens, ukelele-pickin' monsters, a two-headed one-man debate team. It was even nuttier than I'd imagined.

"This is the Muppet wardrobe department," said Kermit, "and here's the lovely Miss Piggy, trying on her new ensemble. Pepe, why don't you show Hockney the Muppet mailroom?"

Hockney protested, "But when do I start rehearsals for my big Muppet television debut?"

"All in good time, Hockney," said Kermit. "Showbiz is kinda like a frog. You gotta start out small, like a tadpole, then swim around in the pond a bit, growing bigger until you're ready to drop your tail, jump up on that lily pad and take the spotlight."

"That's right, tadpole," said Pepe, leading Hockney down the hall. "You gonna just love swimming around in the mailroom, okay. Heh heh!"

"That Hockney is one determined kid. He's kind of bossy," I said.

"Hmmm, well, yes," said Kermit, "I do have some experience with bossy pigs."

DRESSING ROOM

I HEARD THAT!

"Yeesh!" said Kermit. "Excuse me, Danvers. I gotta go do some quick damage control, so I don't get damaged. Piggy! I'm sorry!"

While Kermit ran to Piggy's dressing room, I took a look around the place. It was so cool to see and touch some of my favourite props from classic Muppet comedy bits. There was one of Gonzo's battered trumpets, a laser from "Pigs in Space," and a white and pink polka-dot bow tie—

"Wait a minute!" I said, grabbing the tie. "This is Fozzie Bear's!"

"Hey!" yelped a familiar voice.

Oops! Fozzie's bow tie was still attached to Fozzie Bear! "I'm so sorry, Mr Fozzie, er, uh, Mr Bear!" I stuttered.

"It's okay," said Fozzie. "Please. Call me Fozzie. Have jokes, will travel! Say, have you seen Kermit around?"

"Uh...he's dealing with some steamed pork at the moment," I said. "Is something wrong?"

"It's Gonzo and Rizzo," said Fozzie. "They're in Studio 3D. Come quick!"

Gonzo?!

CHAPTER

10

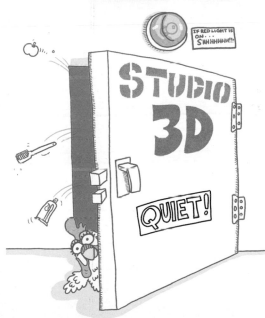

IF RED LIGHT IS ON... SHHHHHH!!!

STUDIO 3D

QUIET!

As Fozzie and I approached the studio

I was a nervous wreck. I was about to meet the greatest entertainer on the planet. I was so wracked with nerves I almost told Fozzie I couldn't go in as he opened the door.

What will Gonzo be like? I wondered.

There he was, dressed as a tube of Rins'N'Spit toothpaste, with a mob of irate rats beating him with giant toothbrushes.

"What's going on here?" I shouted, rushing in to break it up. "I thought you and Rizzo were best friends!"

Gonzo explained the stunt. "I was swinging from tooth to tooth on a trapeze, dressed as a Rins'N'Spit toothpaste tube, annihilating plaque as I went! Rizzo was supposed to catch me when I leapt across the halitosis-laden tongue!"

"I did catch you!" cried Rizzo. "That's the problem! You weigh five times more than me. Just look at my arms! They're stretched out to four feet long!"

I tried to smooth things over. "I'm sure if you guys just take a breather and cool off, you can work this out."

"Nope!" said Rizzo. "I'm done. Finished! Kapooey! Vermin Union rules say I don't have to put up with this kind of treatment! I'm going to work for Miss

Piggy!" shouted Rizzo. "She's been looking for a new assistant since the last one walked out on her. Have you seen the lunch spread in her dressing room? I'll be eating like a king. *Arrivederci*, baby!"

Then Rizzo was out the door.

Gonzo plopped down on a bicuspid. "What am I gonna do now? I've got a whole film crew waiting to finish this commercial."

Suddenly, I had an idea.

"Mr Gonzo, sir?" I said. "I have experience as a trapeze artist. I once performed as half of the Flying Ziti Brothers for my neighbours and immediate family."

Gonzo pondered my offer for a few seconds, then stood up and shouted, "All right, folks! Roll camera and... action!" yelled Gonzo as he swung out over the pulsating tongue.

Then he let go of his trapeze and soared like a scrawny blue bird. I was horrified as he rocketed towards me! I swung out to catch him....

I couldn't believe it! I caught him!

Then the most amazing thing *ever* happened.

Gonzo turned to me and said, "That was great! You're a natural, kid! I want you to be my new assistant! You're like a rat, only taller. Practice starts tomorrow."

Suddenly, my condition didn't seem like such a curse. In fact, it was downright cool.

My parents were happy I had found my dream job, although they were a little freaked out about some of the contracts they had to sign.

But it was a different story when I went to school. Almost everyone there thought I was making the whole trapeze thing up.

Oh, well. They could disbelieve what they wanted to disbelieve about me. I was too happy to care about them. Every day after school, I got to live the dream.

Gonzo and I were working on a stupendous new act. So far, we were making a heck of a team. Every day we came up with groundbreaking performance art. Sometimes Gonzo would even let me make suggestions.

"Danvers," he said while we were taking a snack break, "you must be really popular at your school."

"Actually, I'm kind of considered the school weirdo. No one takes me seriously at all."

Gonzo jumped up. "Really? I have the very same problem! Isn't it great?"

CHAPTER 11

The next day in Mr Piffle's class,

Greevus Snipply held up his phone and played my toothpaste commercial. It was so cool! I had no idea it had gone viral.

When I caught Gonzo at the end of the commercial, the whole class erupted in cheers!

Suddenly everyone wanted my autograph and I was more than happy to give it to them.

Pasquale met me in the hall after class. "Nice trapeze action in that commercial, dude. I hope you stretched properly beforehand and used a safety net."

"It was more like a safety tongue," I said.

Pasquale pulled out a piece of paper. "Hey, I thought you might wanna rehearse some straightjacket escape routines this weekend."

"Sorry, Pasquale, but Kermit's putting together an act for the Fall on Ice Festival. I might get to be in it after all. See ya!"

As I arrived, Kermit was stepping up to the mic to address the packed Muppet auditorium.

"Thank you, Animal and thanks to everyone for showing up! You may have heard that the Muppets have been asked to perform in next week's Fall on Ice Festival! Yaaaaaaay!"

"Oh, Kermie," said Miss Piggy, pushing Kermit aside. "How thoughtful of you to gather everyone here to announce that *moi* will be representing this theatre in *la festival de l'automne*."

"Well, Piggy, there is a *chance* you'll be performing in the festival. I thought it would be fun to have an open audition so everyone could have a shot at performing. You know, a real competition."

Kermit told us we'd have all weekend to rehearse for the audition. I went to find Gonzo. He was in his dressing room with Pepe.

"I'm glad you're here, Danvers!" Gonzo said, opening up an old, rusty safe. "We were just digging out the top secret überstunt that I keep locked away for just this kind of occasion! Okay, according to this we're going to need ten disco dancers on roller skates, five videocassette recorders, a set of encyclopedias, a record player and a dune buggy."

"Uh, how long ago did you lock that stunt away?" I asked.

"Hmmm," Gonzo pondered. "Good question. When was Roosevelt in office?"

"Uh, Gonzo, I don't think any of that stuff is still around. We're gonna need something more up-to-date and current. Something more hip."

"Yeah," said Pepe. "And something that doesn't smell like old dirty cheese, okay."

I decided to tell Gonzo and Pepe the whole tragic

story of my failed audition for the Fall on Ice Festival.

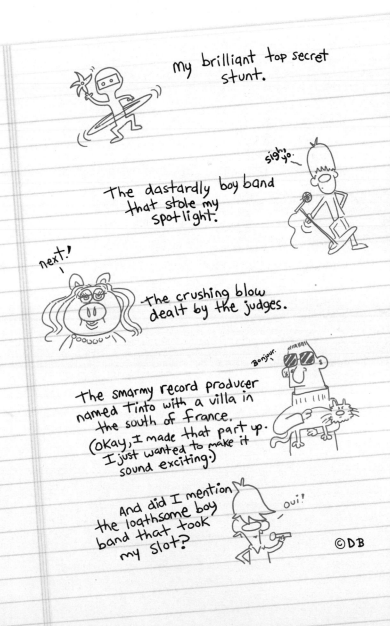

"My point is," I concluded, "because of that sappy boy band, I am still sitting on a stunt so dangerous and so bold that it would have made Harry Houdini seek early retirement. A stunt that I am willing to offer to you, now, in your moment of need."

Gonzo started bouncing up and down with excitement.

"That's a great idea! A boy band! Danvers, you're a genius! While I perform daring acts of bravery, I shall be backed up by an all-new *Muppet Show* boy band! Pepe, go grab some of the other guys!"

I heaved a big sigh. So much for the ninjas.

CHAPTER 12

danvers, the boy genius, has come up with the perfect act for the festival: a muppet boy band! this is so exciting! we're going to need volunteers. fozzie, from now on, we're gonna call you teddy b, and you'll be a backup singer.
okay, just tell me when to stop backing up! wocka! wocka!
DRESSING ROOM
BOY BAND WEEKLY

Gonzo was a barrel of energy as

he assembled his new supergroup.

"Scooter!" he screamed. "You'll be our other backup singer. Since you look vaguely boy-like, you'll be perfect!

"That's great!" said Scooter. "We'll sing barbershop quartet and old-school pep songs, and it will be—"

"Wait a minute!" I yelled. "I can't believe I'm saying this, but if you want to make a successful boy band, you're gonna have to get with the programme. The first thing you gotta do," I said, mussing up my hair, "is comb your hair down over your eyes and wear some baggy clothes."

"Then you gotta say things like 'Girl, you stepped on my heart, yo.' Now you guys try it."

oh, that's smooth.

GIRL! GIRL! GIRL! GIRL! HEART! HEART! HEART! YO! YO! YO! YO!

"Okay," I said with a cough. "Maybe someone other than Animal should be lead singer. The next thing we'll need is a cool name. Something with a lot of angst."

"I've got it!" shouted Gonzo. "I was just looking at this weather map over here and the perfect name for our boy band hit me like a cold front: 'Mon Swoon'!"

I had to admit that "Mon Swoon" was catchy.

"So it's set!" announced Gonzo. "Animal will play the drums, Fozzie and Scooter will do the backup singing and some fancy dance grooves and our lead vocalist will be none other than... Danvers!"

I was shocked. "Me? Really? But Gonzo, what will you do?"

He put on his daredevil helmet and declared, "Dementedly dangerous stunts, of course. We shall be the first group ever to combine death-defying feats of courage with tween-friendly crooning!"

Everyone cheered! I was kind of relieved. For a

minute there I had thought there would be no danger involved.

Back at home, I couldn't decide if I should call Pasquale. How would he feel if he found out I was going to be in a boy band? I just couldn't bring myself to tell him....

Chloe was hitting my bunk with her ball again. I leaned over. "What do you want?" I asked.

"I booked you a big TV interview for tomorrow morning. Don't blow it," she said.

"I wouldn't even know what to say."

Suddenly, Chloe's head appeared at the top of the ladder, and a thick stack of papers landed on my chest. "What the heck is this?" I cried.

"Your script," said Chloe. "Memorize it by dawn. I juiced up some of the boring parts. And get yourself some decent clothes," she added.

CHAPTER 13

My morning TV interview **had** been a complete blur; all I could think about was the audition. Now it was here and I was nervous. This was my second time auditioning for the same show in two weeks and I was shaking like a naked mole rat as I sneaked a peek at the three bigwig judges out there ready to tear us apart.

In addition to the official judges, Statler and Waldorf were up in their box seats.

"All right, people!" yelled Kermit. "Places, everyone! Time for the auditions to begin!"

The auditions were a crazy mix of styles and talent. Lou Zealand was the first to try out, with his boomerang flying-fish act.

He scored great with the judges – until one of his fish mysteriously failed to return.

Sweetums wowed them with a tutu-and-ukelele version of "On Top of Spaghetti."

Then the Swedish Chef took the stage on a dirt bike. Chef revved his motorcycle, then took off across the stage, pulling poor Hockney, who was skiing behind him on roller skates.

Then it was time for the showstopper: the one and only Miss Piggy.

"Kissy kissy!" said Piggy as she was lowered from the ceiling on a gold-plated shopping trolley. "Welcome to the Cabaret Buffet!"

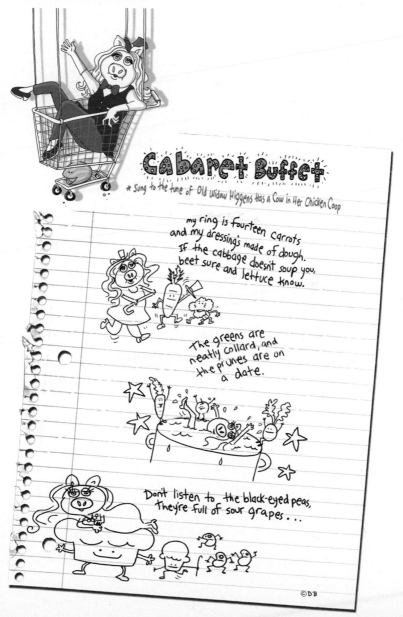

Cabaret Buffet

* Sung to the tune of Old Widow Higgens Has a Cow in Her Chicken Coop

my ring is fourteen carrots
and my dressing's made of dough.
If the cabbage doesn't soup you,
beet sure and lettuce know.

The greens are neatly collard, and the prunes are on a date.

Don't listen to the black-eyed peas, they're full of sour grapes...

©DB

After Miss Piggy's extravaganza, I was super-worried.

"I don't want to be a downer, man, but you guys are doomed, okay," said Pepe.

"How are we supposed to follow that?" worried Fozzie.

"With gusto!" shouted Gonzo, leaping out in a red, white and blue jumpsuit and helmet. "Come on, fellas! Let's knock their socks off!"

I slid out onstage with the rest of the band and before I knew it, the curtain was raised and Kermit ran out to introduce us.

"Ladies and gentlemen, let's give a big warm-with-a-chance-of-showers welcome to Mon Swoon!"

Camilla and her chicken friends clucked and clapped for us as I grabbed the mic.

We rocked the house! I swear I saw the judges tapping their feet – even Sam the Eagle. I was starting to see the appeal of being in a boy band. It was actually pretty fun.

Fozzie and Scooter showed off some slick dance moves and Animal tore it up on the drums, although his ten-minute solo *was* a bit much.

The best part was in the middle of the song, when Gonzo came blazing in on rocket-powered roller skates, playing a saxophone that shot flames! Unfortunately it shot the flames right into the stage curtains and they

went up like a bonfire

"Keep playing!" I told the others as Kermit and Pepe blasted the curtains with a fire extinguisher.

When the song was over and the fire was out, the judges and crowd gave us a standing ovation.

At the end of the auditions, Kermit had all the contestants gather onstage for the big announcement. Miss Piggy stayed close to Kermit so she could swiftly sweep in to give her acceptance speech.

"By a unanimous decision," said Kermit, "the winner is... Mon Swoon! Yaaaaaaay!"

I couldn't believe it. We did it! I was going to play in the Fall on Ice Festival!

CHAPTER 14

We had one week until the big

festival and even though she didn't win the audition, I knew Miss Piggy was the expert on being a celebrity and she was cool enough to give us some pointers. (Okay, so we paid her, but at least she didn't hurt us!)

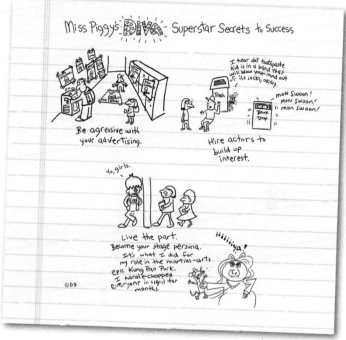

I followed her tips to the letter.

I combed my hair down over my eyes, got some fancy baggy clothes and practised talking like a smooth operator.

There were a lot of haters out there, but I didn't let them get me down.

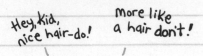

Even Pasquale seemed totally irritated with me for some reason. He had pretty much just stopped hanging out with me. One day during lunch, I caught him palling around with my mortal enemy, Kip Strummer!

"What are you doing, Pasquale?" I said, pulling him aside. "That guy's such a phony. Not to mention he's jealous of my new lead-singer gig. We're better than him and his pack of tween heartthrobs."

"I'm not so sure about that," said Pasquale. "Like my mother's always telling my little brother, 'Kid, you're going through a phase and you better snap out of it quick.'"

To make matters worse, Kip and Danny Enfant walked up to us.

"Hey, Danvers," said Kip. "Congrats on the big musical gig. Maybe we should get together and jam sometime?"

"Oh, please," I snapped. "You just want to see what Mon Swoon has in store for the big show!"

Pasquale just shook his head at me and walked away. "Come on, guys," he said to Kip and Danny.

I'm not sure, but it really seemed like my best friend was turning his back on me in my moment of glory.

Whatever. I was the lead singer of Mon Swoon.

CHAPTER 15

I tried to shrug off the bummer

that was school when I went to the Muppet Theatre that afternoon. Gonzo was adding a killer loop-de-loop wooden ramp stunt to our act.

"Check this out, Danvers!" he said, spreading out his blueprints. "While you guys sing your hearts out, I will rocket down this icy ramp on jet-propelled ice skates, zoom through this harrowing loop, launch into the air like a majestic turkey vulture and zap some sort of hurled fruit with my saxophone."

"Ahem!" Kermit coughed, clearing his throat. "Gonzo, I'm afraid I can't allow the flame-throwing saxophone."

"Never fear, *el jefe*! I've replaced the flame-throwing sax with one that shoots liquid nitrogen. It'll temporarily freeze anything it hits."

"Oops," said Gonzo. "Don't worry. Frozen shrimp only takes a few minutes to thaw."

> i...am not...a shrimp...
> i ammm...a king...prawn...okay.

All of a sudden, Fozzie ran in, saying, "Hey, Danvers! You're on TV!"

I had totally forgotten about my big TV interview. We all crammed into Kermit's office to watch his little TV.

"...Here Danvers sits with his loving and supportive family. Just look at his adorable sister, Chloe."

"But when we interviewed some of Danvers's friends, a different story emerged."

> i kinda miss the old danvers, from before he became a famous musician. we used to do crazy stunts. now he only does them with gonzo - that is, when he's not singing with his boy band saying "yo" all the time....we don't ever hang out anymore.

"You did that to your friend?" asked Pepe. "How could you? That sounds like something I would do!"

"Wow," I said. "I was all excited to see myself on TV. I didn't know Pasquale still wanted to do stunts – I've been totally ignoring my best friend! I treated him like dirt."

Kermit patted me on the back, saying, "Danvers, you've made some real friends in this old theatre and we're glad to have you here, but you can't forget your other buddies. Especially your best friend. You gotta make it right."

"But Pasquale's so upset with me," I said. "What do I do?"

"Apologize," said Rizzo, bursting into the room. "Just go over there and say you're sorry. The longer you sit on it, the harder it'll get. In fact, I've got someone to apologize to! Gonzo, I can't believe I'm saying this, but I'm sorry I acted like such a baby!"

"And I'm sorry I stretched out your arms like saltwater taffy!" Gonzo cried.

They hugged and sobbed and blew their noses into each other's shirts.

I stood up and declared, "You're right, guys! I'm going to tell Pasquale I'm sorry!"

"Well, it's settled, then," said Kermit. "Danvers, go pay Pasquale a little visit and then you better get some rest. That goes for all of you! We've got a big show tomorrow!"

I rushed over to Pasquale's house and knocked on his window. Curtis was my wingman, riding on my shoulder with his claws securely hooked in my felt to offer support and guidance.

Pasquale opened the window and looked down at me, wrapped in his blanket.

"Hey, your hair's back to normal," he noticed.

"Yeah, I mussed it up. I was tired of looking like my Aunt Patty. Hey, Pasquale—"

Pasquale waved his hand. "You don't gotta say anything. I can already see I'm looking at the old Danvers, even if you do have orange skin and a bright red, removable nose."

"I don't know what happened," I said. "With all this crazy stuff goin' on, my brain just got all..."

"Discombobulated?"

"Discombobulated!" I nodded. "That's the perfect word for it."

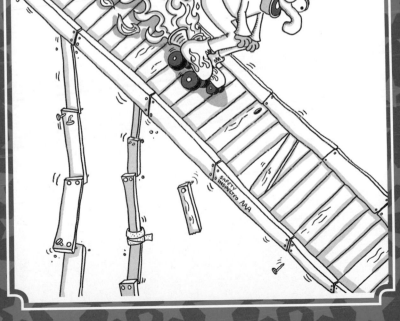

Saturday was packed solid with rehearsals for our song and Gonzo's loop-de-loop liquid-nitrogen stunt. The Fall on Ice Festival would start at the Block City Coliseum at seven thirty, so we had a few more hours to get it just right. I even asked Pasquale to be the safety supervisor, and Curtis helped out by gnawing on Fozzie.

thanks. i needed a little trim off the top.

Kermit was frantically running around getting ready, but he kindly took the time to introduce himself to Pasquale.

"Nice to meet you," he said. "From all that Danvers has told me, you are a true pal – Look out!!!"

We all jumped out of the way just in the nick of time as Gonzo blazed through the room on his rocket-powered roller skates. He crashed headfirst into Camilla's chicken coop, setting off an explosion of feathers. I could see Pasquale already taking notes about what safety equipment Gonzo should be using.

"Dr Honeydew is on line two for Danvers. He says it's, like, urgent or something." Janice held up the phone for me.

I ran over and grabbed it. I could hear bleeps and blips and frantic meeps! on the line. "Hello, this is Danvers speaking."

Then the line went dead.

I hung up the phone and looked at the time. Six o'clock!

After I explained what was going on, Kermit patted my shoulder and said, "You'd better get over there, pronto! You guys need to be back here by seven to catch the bus over to the show!"

I turned to Gonzo and asked, "But what if Dr Honeydew changes me back to a regular boring old sixth grader? No offense, Pasquale."

"I don't care if you come back as Mary Poppins!" said Gonzo. "Just get here by seven to catch the bus to the show!"

CHAPTER 17

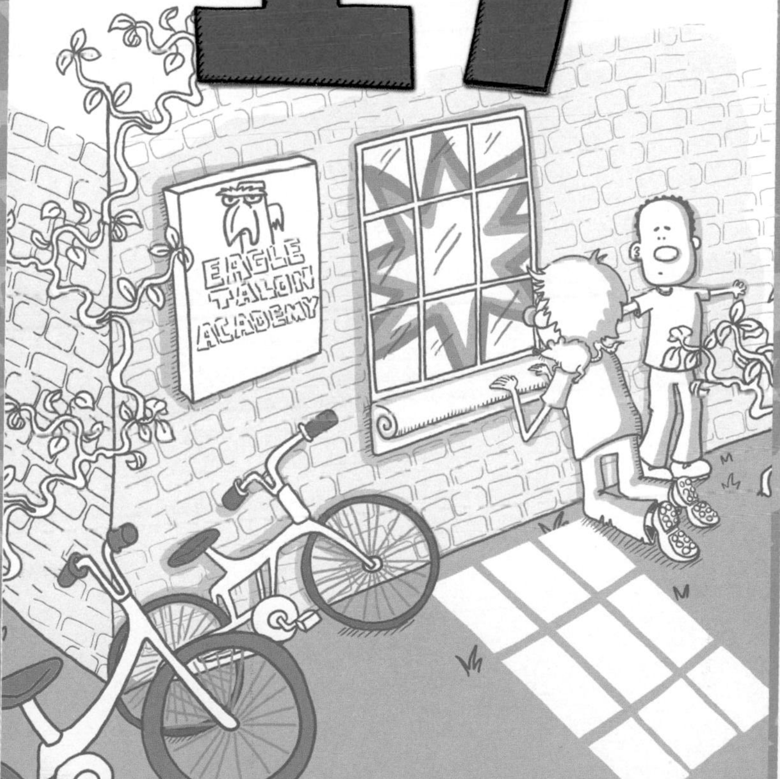

We pedalled our bikes over to Eagle Talon Academy. The place was deserted and dark, except for a creepy green glow coming from Dr Honeydew's lab.

Inside the science lab, Honeydew and Beaker were tinkering with a gigantic metal laser cannon.

"Oh, greetings, young science pioneers! Beaker and I were just putting the finishing touches on the SHAMPUZ laser. Since the device is powered by an unstable plutonium triple-A battery, we only have a short window in which to fire it at young Danvers's head. Beaker and I restored the laser to working order, then I reversed the polarity on the gyroscopic invertosphere and triggered the ionic plu—"

"English, Dr Honeydew!" I yelled. "In English, please!"

"Oh," he said. "Well, I switched that whatchamacallit on that thingy there and flipped this thingamabobber to point at that doohickey over there."

"Will it work?" asked Pasquale.

"Theoretically, maybe."

Pasquale shouted, "Dude! You can't just let him zap you with a dangerous radioactive laser beam!"

"Squeak! Squeak!" Curtis chirped in agreement.

Pasquale and Curtis had a good point. What was I doing letting some wacky scientist blast me with radiation? And besides, did I really want to go back to the old Danvers?

Curtis and Pasquale looked at me with trembling fear in their eyes.

"Sorry, guys," I said. "But I'm gonna go for it. I've got to be me. It's a chance I've got to take."

"I think you're crazy," Pasquale said with a sigh.

The digital readout on the laser cannon started to count down and the whole contraption began to rumble. Pasquale ran and ducked behind a desk, while I made sure I was standing right in the line of fire. A glowing green light, just like the one I had seen before, filled the room and an ear-piercing metallic screech bombarded my eardrums. Suddenly, a ghastly green laser shot out of the cannon and just as it was about to zap my noggin –

ZAPPO!

Curtis jumped up and blocked its path! The poor little guy took the brunt of the blast. The laser sputtered out and the green light faded away, leaving the room full of smoke. When it cleared, Honeydew examined Curtis with a magnifying glass. He was fine. "That was quite anticlimactic, I'm afraid."

I couldn't believe Curtis had jumped in front of a laser for me. Anything could have happened. "Why did you do it, Curtis?"

"He didn't want you getting hurt," said Pasquale. "That's one faithful rat."

"And he didn't even transform," I said, scratching Curtis under his chin.

"For now," said Dr Honeydew. "The transformation could occur gradually. Perhaps overnight, like in your case. Watch him closely. In a few hours it could be a different story."

"A few hours!" I yelped, looking at the clock. "Pasquale, we've got fifteen minutes to get to the bus or they'll leave without us!"

We hopped on our bikes and pedalled like mad.

CHAPTER 18

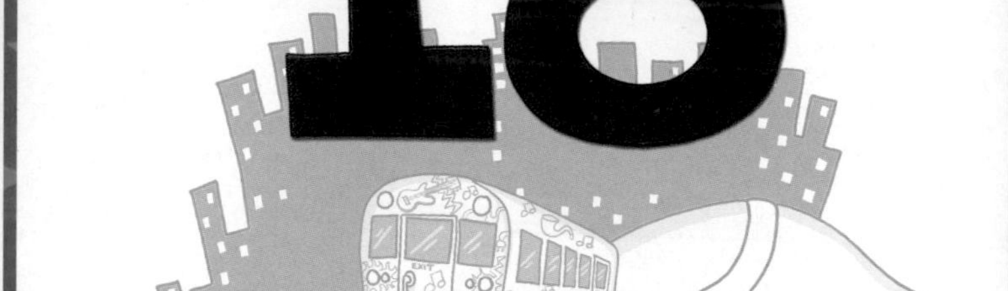

The bus was pulling away from the theatre as we rode up. I waved wildly to get their attention.

"Sorry we're late," I apologized as we climbed aboard the Muppet-packed bus.

"No harm, no foul," said Dr Teeth. "All right, *los pasajeros*! Fasten your safety belts and keep your arms, legs and egos in the vehicle at all times!"

Dr Teeth stepped on the gas and the bus took off like a high-speed bullet train.

"Whoa!" said Pasquale, pointing at my shoulder. "Curtis is getting fat!"

Actually, I thought he *was* feeling kind of heavier than normal. I picked him up and held him close to inspect him. I couldn't believe my eyes. Curtis was the size of a raccoon and he was getting bigger by the second!

Pasquale grabbed my arm. "I don't think Dr Honeydew's laser turns things into Muppets – it turns them into giant monsters!"

Floyd pulled out a pet carrier and said, "Here! Use this. It's the 'mobile tranquility room' we put Animal in when he needs a time-out."

I grabbed a salted snack treat from Hockney and used it to lure Curtis into the carrier, then slammed the door shut.

I gave Dr Honeydew a call and filled him in on our giant rat problem.

I tried to pet Curtis through the mesh door, but he snapped at me. The pet carrier was starting to bulge at the seams – soon he'd be too big for it.

"Don't worry, Danvers," said Gonzo. "I'm sure Dr Honeydew will get him back to normal."

"Hang in there, Curtis," I said with a sigh. "After the show, we'll get you right as rain."

CHAPTER 19

The Fall on Ice Festival was a star-studded extravaganza. The red carpet had been rolled out, spotlights were crisscrossing in the night sky and everyone attending got a Block City Coliseum collectible backscratcher. The city had spared no expense.

Being such huge stars, Kermit and Miss Piggy got to walk the carpet and they invited me and Pasquale to tag along. I couldn't believe all the celebs we spotted.

"I wonder what huge star we'll spot next?" I whispered to Pasquale. Out of the blue, a whole stampede of reporters rushed towards us. Miss Piggy flipped her hair and struck a pose, saying, "Ooooh, they're coming this way, Kermie! Quick, get behind me and fluff my hair!"

But the reporters passed right by Miss Piggy and jammed their cameras and microphones in my face. I got bombarded with all kinds of crazy questions.

The mob was relentless and I couldn't get past them. I lost Pasquale when he got swallowed up by the crowd. Even Kermit and Piggy got pushed along the red carpet. Then, all of a sudden, I spotted my family on the sidelines. I grabbed my little sister and plopped her in front of the reporters.

"Here!" I announced. "It's the real-life little sister of Danvers, the boy wonder! Isn't she adorable?"

While they pounced on her with questions, I managed to dart into the theatre.

As I looked at the audience inside the theatre, it seemed like everyone was there.

There were Mr Piffle and Coach Kraft. Sam the Eagle was there with the Swedish Chef. Statler and Waldorf were there too.

Then I noticed the girls from Eagle Talon Academy, Ingy and Minette, and – Wait a minute! Pasquale was over there, flirting with them.

"Pasquale!" I interrupted. "We have to get backstage! Our act is going on soon!"

Just then, Kip Strummer took to the ice with his band. Everyone in the crowd went nuts as he skated a figure eight on the ice, then did a triple Lutz into a double Axel. All the girls in the audience exhaled at once and almost melted the ice.

Kip grabbed the mic and said, "Thank you. I learned that little trick in Calgary. This first song goes out to you, girl, and only you. And when I say only you, I mean every one of you. It's called 'Girl, You Froze My Heart Then Melted It with a Flamethrower, Yo.'"

"*Pourquoi, fille? Pourquoi?*" said Danny.

Their song gave me mixed emotions – it made me want to groove and barf at the same time.

"Danvers!" screamed a voice from the side of the ice rink. It was Fozzie, and he looked frantic.

"Get back here, you two! Mon Swoon's on next!"

After practising on roller skates for days, we were finally switching over to the real deal – ice skates! Pasquale was helping me lace mine up when I noticed the pet carrier in the corner. Dr Honeydew and Beaker were examining Curtis through the bars. He was not happy in there and the whole carrier was about to burst open.

"Dr Honeydew! You made it!" I said. "So, what is your expert opinion?"

"Well, I brought a miniature prototype version of the SHAMPUZ laser. I may be able to reverse the accelerated growth, but it's going to be difficult gathering enough power to operate it."

"Meep!" Beaker chirped, fitting a clunky, beeping contraption onto the laser. Then he pulled out a Styrofoam to-go box and poured its cheesy, greasy contents into the top of the device.

"What's that?" I asked.

"We are going to attempt to power the laser by putting Beaker's leftover olive grotto three-cheese-and-sausage fetuccine into this subatomic food processor."

Rizzo ran in and screamed, "All right, guys. It's showtime!"

Kermit grabbed the mic and gave us a sterling introduction: "Ladies and gentlemen, I'm proud to present to you the perfect combination of soulful singing and painful stunt work. Let's give a big warm welcome to Mon Swooooooooon! Yaaaaaay!"

We glided out onto the ice and took our positions near the flimsy wooden loop Gonzo had constructed.

This is crazy, I thought. *Look at the size of this crowd.* Up until that night, the biggest audience I had ever played for fit comfortably in our backyard.

I strummed my guitar and sang my heart out. The crowd loved it! This was my moment. I was living the dream.

CHAPTER 20

It was time for Gonzo's big entrance.

He was standing on top of a huge downhill ramp decked out in his helmet and daredevil duds.

"Pasquale! Hurl the melons!" Gonzo announced.

Pasquale skated out onto the ice with an armload of honeydews and tossed them high into the air. Gonzo rocketed down the ramp on his jet-propulsion skates, tootling a rockin' sax solo.

He blasted through the loop-de-loop and went up another ramp, launching into the air. He was preparing to douse the airborne honeydews with liquid nitrogen when...

"Look out!" shrieked Rizzo.

A gargantuan, woolly mammoth–sized Curtis slid out onto the rink and batted Gonzo to the ice with his paws! The audience screamed in terror as Curtis bellowed a horrifying... SQUEAK!

"Are you okay, Gonzo?" I called out.

"Yeah," he whispered. "Keep playing! Act like this is just part of the show! We don't want to cause a panic!"

So I kept on singing as Rizzo slid a chair and bullwhip out to Gonzo and he used them to hold back the beast like a lion tamer.

The crowd erupted in cheers as Gonzo whipped the monster and bellowed, "Back! Back, *Rodantus giganticus!*"

But Curtis was too much rat for just one Gonzo. He tore apart the wooden loop.

Gonzo grabbed the saxophone and prepared to blow on it. "This one goes out to all the fine chickens out there!"

Gonzo wailed on that horn like a New Orleans jazz master and it blasted liquid nitrogen all over Curtis, who creaked to a halt as he froze up.

"Dr Honeydew!" I called out. "Quick! Zap him before he thaws out!"

Beaker skated out onto the rink holding Dr Honeydew up in an impressive one-handed lift. Honeydew aimed and fired the green laser at Curtis. The entire auditorium lit up with a pulsating green light.

With one last huge blast of green electricity, the coliseum went dark. Then the smoke slowly cleared, revealing a tiny little rat munching on a piece of honeydew melon rind as if nothing had happened.

Gonzo skated to the centre of the rubble-scattered rink and announced, "*Espectáculo finito!*" then bowed like a master matador.

that's odd. i smell the aroma of three-cheese fetuccine.

The whole crowd gave us a standing ovation, then rushed out onto the ice. We were mobbed by reporters, fans and our parents.

Kermit patted both me and Pasquale on the back. "You know, Gonzo was just telling me that with all the publicity this has gotten him, he's going to need a team of assistants. We have room for another intern."

"That's right," added Gonzo. "Pasquale, I'd like you to join Rizzo and Danvers as my road crew! What d'ya say?"

"Really?" Pasquale beamed. "I'd be honoured! Although there are some papers my parents might make you sign first."

Dr Honeydew and Beaker were packing up their laser.

"So, I guess your laser had nothing to do with my Muppet transformation, huh?" I said.

"Looks that way," said Honeydew. "I'm afraid it was just a coincidence that the stray laser blast occurred that night at twelve twenty-two AM."

"I sure hope it didn't hit anything important, or dangerous," worried Pasquale.

CHAPTER

21

is this even meat?

You would have thought that runaway popularity and massive fame awaited me at school the following Monday, but really, it was just business as usual. Mr Piffle was still giving me D's. Mrs Grumbles was still passing over my exciting drama-class ideas. And Coach Kraft was still testing the limits of my endurance.

"I don't know, Pasquale," I said, sighing. "Here I am, still flunking the sixth grade, no girls will talk to me, I'm still eating Gladys's terrible cafeteria food and I have no idea what caused my Muppetmorphosis. I mean, what was that green flash and where did it come from?"

Pasquale tried to cheer me up. "Don't worry about it. At least we've got the Muppet internship after school."

"Yeah, I guess you're right. I just feel like there has to be a reason this all happened."

"Hey, Danvers!" yelled a voice from behind us. It was Kip and he had a couple of his bandmates and swooning girl followers with him. Kip was the last person I wanted to talk to.

"Hey, Kip," I groaned. "What's up?"

"Not much, dude," Kip said, and then he leaned in to whisper in my ear. "Look, I was wondering, can you make me a copy of that report you did on Gonzo? You know, the one about him being your hero? It would really impress my peeps, if you know what I mean."

I looked over at his friends and they all gave me a wave.

"Uh, sure, I guess," I said.

"Thanks, dude!" Kip beamed, walking away. "You know, we should do some kind of act together, like old times. Maybe a music and crazy daredevil stunt hybrid or something. It'd be cool, you know?"

"Yeah," I said. "Hey, wait a minute.... Does this mean Gonzo is *your* hero too?"

Kip laughed and said, "Are you kiddin'? Gonzo is everybody's hero!"

He's right, I thought to myself. After seeing him defeat a five-ton angry rat using rocket-powered ice skates, a whip, five honeydew melons, a wooden chair, a saxophone that sprayed liquid nitrogen and a laser powered by fettuccini, it was abundantly clear to me that Gonzo wasn't just my hero, he was everybody's hero.

Please, discuss among yourselves.